Noddy and the Pirates

Noddy and his friends were at the harbour.
Noddy was very excited because Whiz had a
special surprise for him.

Whiz was very excited too!
"You can open your eyes now, Noddy."

4

"Wow! Fantastic! A Jet Ski!"
Noddy cried in delight. "And in
my colours, too. Thank you."

Whiz was very pleased that
Noddy liked his present.

Just then, Noddy heard a splash.
It was his friends, the mermaids.

"What are you doing?" Noddy asked.

"We're diving for pretty pink pearls,"
the mermaids told him.

The mermaids had collected a lot of pearls.
"We've almost filled our treasure chest," they said, happily.

Noddy told the mermaids he was off to see the pirates.
They waved, as he sped off on his Jet Ski.

Soon, Noddy reached the pirate ship. "Ahoy there,
Noddy and a yo ho ho to Bumpy," the pirates called out.

"Come aboard
and play, arrr!"

10

The pirates welcomed Noddy and Bumpy
on board with a funny song and dance.

"I bet being a pirate is really good fun," said Noddy.

"Arrr! How would you and Bumpy like to be pirates
for the day?" the pirates asked.

"We'd love it!" Noddy cheered.

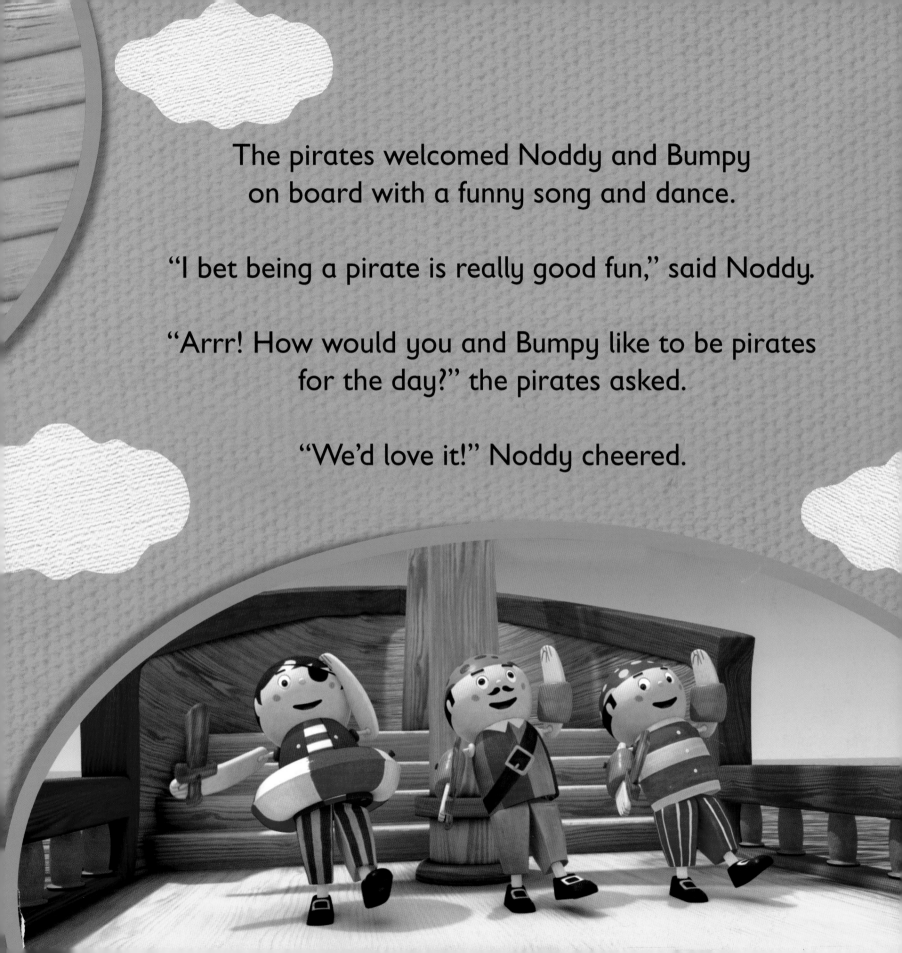

"What else do pirates do?" asked Noddy.

"That's it really…" said the pirates, looking confused.

Noddy realised he would have to teach them everything he knew!

"Pirates wear eye patches, have parrots on their shoulders and bury treasure," Noddy told them.

The pirates liked the sound of treasure. They chorused,

"Yeah!"

Noddy and the pirates jumped in a rowing boat and set off to search for hidden treasure.

"Land ahoy!"

Noddy cried, as he spotted a tiny island in the distance.

Noddy found some small stones
and showed them to the pirates.

"Look pirates, silver coins," he pretended.
"Let's get digging, mateys!"

With Bumpy's help, Noddy and the pirates
soon buried the silver coins.

"Noddy, how do pirates know where they've buried
their treasure?" the pirates asked.

"They draw treasure maps," said Noddy, holding one up
for the pirates to see. "X marks the spot."

15

"Let's bury some more treasure!"
the pirates cheered.

So Noddy and Bumpy ran off to collect some
big shells that looked like shiny gold plates.

16

But when Noddy and Bumpy
came back, the pirates were gone.
Noddy spotted them in the rowing boat.

"Where are they going?" Noddy wondered.
Then he saw a treasure chest on the shore.

"Oh no!" Noddy cried. "The mermaids' pearls!"

Noddy watched as the pirates picked up the treasure chest and carried it away.

"The pirates are going to bury the pearls, but how are we going to get off this island to stop them?" Noddy wondered.

Suddenly, Noddy had an idea.
They could use the big shell as a boat!

"Full speed ahead, Bumpy!"

Noddy cried, as they splashed through the
water towards the pirates.

19

But Noddy arrived too late, the pirates had already buried the treasure!

"You can't take other people's things without asking," Noddy explained.

"Sorry, Noddy, we were just pirating around," the pirates said.

"Don't worry," Noddy told his friends. "If we dig up the chest, we can return it before the mermaids know it's gone."

Everyone started digging as fast as they could.

"Ahoy, Noddy! I think the mermaids are coming back," shouted one of the pirates.

"Quick!" cried Noddy. "Here it is!"

Noddy and the pirates took hold of the treasure chest and pulled as hard as they could. "Heave ho!" they chorused.

23

The treasure chest flew out of the sand and landed on the shore, just as the mermaids arrived with more pearls.

"Now the treasure chest is full!" they said.

Everyone was happy. The pirates had learned how to be pirates, the mermaids had collected lots of treasure, and Noddy and Bumpy Dog had enjoyed lots and lots of fun!

The Magic Watering Can

It was a hot, sunny day and
Noddy was helping Big Ears in the
garden at Toadstool House.

"It's kind of you to help me
on such a warm day, Noddy,"
said Big Ears, gratefully.

"That's okay, Big Ears,
this is fun!" said Noddy, as he
used his watering can to water
all the pretty plants.

29

Even Bumpy wanted to help.
He ran round and round the garden.

"Oh, Bumpy!" laughed Noddy.
"Try not to dig too many holes!"

Bumpy decided to have a rest,
as it was such a sunny day.

"All this sun and water must be good for your plants,
Big Ears – they're really great!" said Noddy.

"I give them a little help with my magic watering can,"
said Big Ears. "I never use too much magic, though!"

31

Noddy watched in amazement as the plants sprung up from little shoots to lovely, big flowers.

"That's magic!"

gasped Noddy. "What a wonderful watering can you have, Big Ears."

It was such a hot day, that Noddy decided to
buy some lemonade to take to Tessie's.

It seemed like everyone in Toyland
had the same idea! They all wanted a nice cold drink,
as it was so warm and sunny.

"Lots of cool lemonade, please,
Mr Wobbly Man," said Noddy.

"Brrr!
That's perfect!"

Just then, Mr Jumbo appeared.
"I'd like a lemonade, too, please!" he bellowed.

"Coming up!" said Mr Wobbly Man.
"Why don't you sit in the shade while you drink it?"

"There's not much shade to fit under," said Mr Jumbo,
flapping his ears to keep cool.

38

When Noddy arrived at Tessie's house,
they sat down to enjoy their drinks.

"This lemonade is a lovely surprise, Noddy,"
said Tessie. "You must try some of my fairy cakes.
They'll be ready soon."

"Fairy cakes! Yum! Oh, and I have another
surprise for you, Tessie!" said Noddy.

Noddy waved Big Ears' magic watering can in the air.
"It's MAGIC, Tessie!" said Noddy. "Watch this!"

Noddy started to sprinkle water all over
Tessie's pretty tomato plants.

The plants didn't seem to get any bigger,
so Noddy kept on watering them.

"Hmmm…it worked for Big Ears," he said, with a
puzzled look. "Perhaps they need even more water."

Noddy kept on sprinkling.
Then suddenly, Tessie's tomato plants started to

grow...
    and grow...
        and GROW!

41

"Oh no, Noddy," said Tessie. "The plants are so big they are blocking my door and my fairy cakes are still baking in the oven!"

"Don't worry, Tessie!" cried Noddy. "I've got a big Noddy plan!"

He called for Lindy and Car.

42

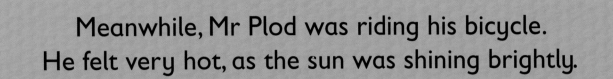

Meanwhile, Mr Plod was riding his bicycle.
He felt very hot, as the sun was shining brightly.

"Phew! What a scorcher," he said, as he pedalled.
Just then, he spotted the very big plant in front of Tessie's
house. He turned his head and stared…

Crash! Boing! Splash!

Mr Plod toppled off his bicycle and into the pond!

"Well, that's cooled me down a bit!" he chuckled.
"But what's little Noddy up to now?"

Noddy was climbing up the tomato plant,
which was now as big as a tree.

He looked down and saw that Lindy had arrived to help him.

"I'm going to start cutting away the leaves so that Tessie can get into her house," Noddy explained. "Car will catch them for me!"

"Good idea, Noddy!"

45

said Lindy, as she hovered next to him.

When Noddy had finished, he climbed back down to Tessie. Big Ears had just arrived.

"I wanted to warn you not to use too much of my watering can's magic, Noddy," said Big Ears. "But I think I'm too late!"

"Don't worry, Big Ears," said Noddy. "The extra-big leaves are very useful on this hot and sunny day!"

46

The giant leaves made great parasols for
all the Toy Town friends.

"I'm nice and cool now," said Mr Jumbo, as he held up his leaf.

Dinah Doll, the Skittles and Clockwork Mouse all agreed.
"Clever, Noddy!" they said, as they stayed cool.

Tessie was very happy,
as her fairy cakes were saved!
But what were they going to do
with the giant tomatoes that had
piled up outside?

"I have an idea!" said Noddy,
"We'll have a spaghetti party!"

So they sat down and shared a
plate of tasty spaghetti.

Slurp!
Yum!
Slurp!

"What delicious tomato sauce!"
they both agreed.

49

Hide-and-Seek Fun

The sun was shining brightly in Toyland. Noddy, Tessie and Bumpy Dog were having lots of fun playing hide-and-seek.

"I love playing hide-and-seek,"

Noddy said, "but it's even better with more people."
So the friends set off to see if anyone else wanted to play.

52

Meanwhile, in the garage, Whiz and Lindy were hard at work.

Lindy needed to move a big engine, but it was too heavy to lift.

Whiz knew how to help his friend. "We will use the big
magnet," he told Lindy. "It attracts metal things."

Whiz pressed a button on the remote control, but the big
magnet was more powerful than
Whiz realised…

"Lindy! Turn it off!"

Whiz cried, as Noddy
was pulled into the garage. The magnet
had attracted the jingling bell on his hat!

Lindy pressed a button. "Not that button!"
Whiz shouted, but it was too late.

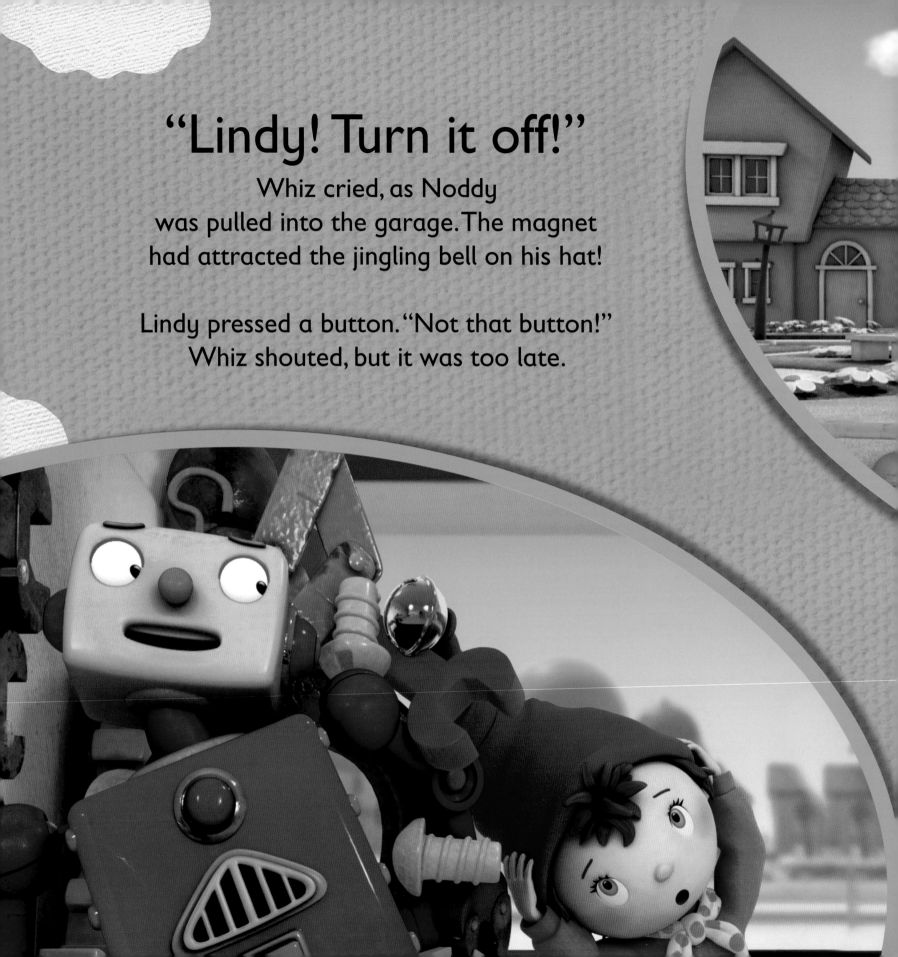

The magnet gathered up all of the metal things in the
garage and dumped them outside!

"Ha, ha," laughed Noddy, as he landed on the ground
with a bump. "I called to see if you wanted to
play hide-and-seek," he said to Whiz.

55

Whiz had never heard of hide-and-seek, so Noddy explained the rules.

"You hide and wait for a friend to find you," he told Whiz. "You need to make sure it's a good place to hide. Somewhere difficult to find," Noddy added.

"What a fascinating game. I'd love to play!" Whiz declared.

"Go ahead, Whiz," Lindy told her friend. "I'll look after the garage."

56

Noddy shut his eyes tightly
and began to count to 20.

"One, two, three…"

Whiz set off down the road to find
somewhere to hide.

"A quick scan of my memory bank has located an
excellent hiding place," he said to himself. "Beep!"

Whiz was so excited, he didn't notice he was getting
in the way of the cars behind him.

Bang!

Jumbo swerved to avoid Whiz and drove
straight into a lamp post!

"Oh no, a scratch on my pride and joy!" he cried.

But Whiz hadn't noticed the damage he'd caused,
he was too busy racing to his hiding place!

Soon, Whiz had left Toy Town far behind him.

"Almost there!" he said, as he crossed a little bridge,
beeping happily.

Meanwhile, Noddy was busy searching for his friends.

"No one in there," he said,
peering inside the ice cream parlour.

61

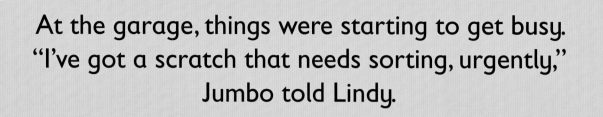

At the garage, things were starting to get busy.
"I've got a scratch that needs sorting, urgently,"
Jumbo told Lindy.

"And I need winding up," squeaked Clockwork Mouse.
Lindy couldn't do all of this by herself.
She needed Whiz.

Just then, Noddy appeared.
"Have you found Whiz yet?" Lindy asked him.

"No, he's the last one," Noddy told her.
"He's very good at hiding!"

Lindy didn't know what to do, but Noddy had an idea.
"I know! We'll use the magnet to find him!"

63

Noddy's idea was very clever.
He tied the magnet to his
helicopter and set off to
search for Whiz,
with Bumpy at his side.

Noddy knew that Whiz was
made of metal, so the
magnet would attract him!

Tessie jumped in her
car to join the search.

65

High up in the sky, Noddy could
see all around him.

"It doesn't look like Whiz is anywhere
close by," he said to Bumpy.

"Try turning the magnet up to full power,"
Noddy shouted to Tessie, who was driving below him.

Tessie turned the dial.

If this didn't work, would they ever find Whiz?

67

"I enjoyed my first
game of hide-and-seek,"
Whiz told Noddy.

"You were really good
at it," Noddy praised.
"Too good for me!"

"Next time I'll hide
somewhere a little closer,"
Whiz said.

That sounds like
a good idea!

A Very Special Birthday

Whiz and Lindy were hard at
work in the garage when Noddy
and Tessie called by.

74

"I've been checking my book
of Toy Town birthdays and
yours isn't in it!" Lindy told Whiz.

"It is because robots do not have
birthdays," Whiz explained. "We just
have lots and lots of work days."

Noddy didn't think this sounded very fair.
Suddenly, he had an idea.
"Let's make today your birthday!" he cried.

"Oh, that's a great idea!" agreed Tessie.

"Beep!"

said Whiz. "Thank you, but what is a birthday?"

Lindy couldn't believe Whiz didn't know! "It's when you get a year older," she explained. "And you get birthday cards and a birthday present!"

Whiz thought birthdays sounded lots of fun.

"I feel so happy and excited!"
he cried, as he rolled out of the
garage and down the street.

"Bzzt! Buzz! Beep!"

Everyone was so busy watching Whiz, they didn't notice
the naughty goblins hiding round the corner.

"There's some horrible birthday fun going on around here,"
Sly told Gobbo, looking at his funometer.
"And what is goblin rule number one?"

"Always try and spoil the fun!"
Sly and Gobbo cackled together.

Just then, Mr Plod arrived at the garage.
"Now we can play some party games,"
Noddy cheered. "This one's called pass the parcel."

"My favourite!" laughed Mr Plod.

Whiz looked puzzled as the friends passed the parcel.
"Nobody seems to like this parcel," he said to Noddy.

"No, Whiz, you're supposed to keep passing
it until the music stops!" Noddy chuckled.
"Then you unwrap it."

"Oh, I did not know that," Whiz told him.

Sly and Gobbo were still spying on the friends.
"Ha, ha, Whiz doesn't know what to do!" laughed Gobbo.

"Yes, so we could tell him anything," added Sly, with a grin.

When Noddy and the others left the garage
to plan a surprise party for Whiz,
the goblins saw their chance to make mischief!

"Happy birthday!"

Sly cried, as he crept up on Whiz.

"Noddy forgot to tell you about some other important fun things that happen on birthdays."

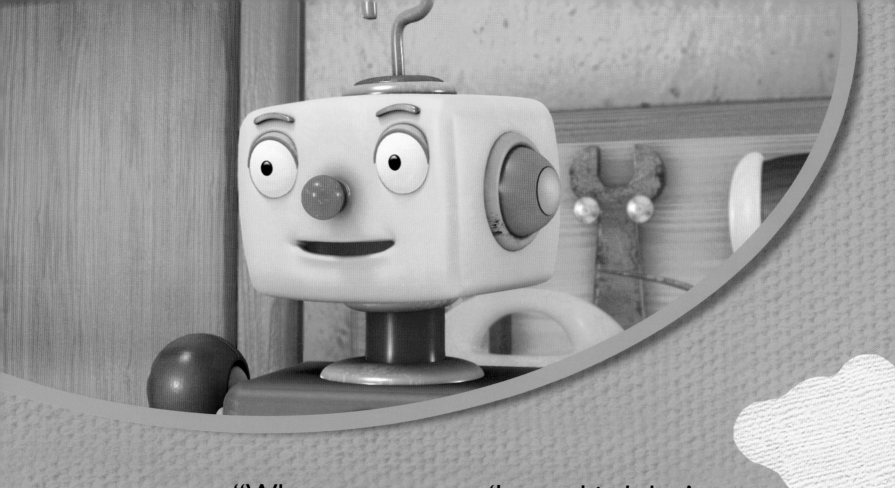

"When anyone says 'happy birthday'
you have to crow like a cockerel," Sly fibbed.

"Cock-a-doodle-do!"

crowed Gobbo.

"And you should eat your birthday cards," added Sly.

"Goodness, I thought we'd be eating party food,"
said Whiz in surprise.

"What about his birthday present, Sly?"
asked Gobbo.

"It's normal to throw it away," said Sly.
"Out to sea if possible!"

Sly nudged Gobbo. "Well, if that doesn't spoil the party,
I don't know what will!" he whispered.

Meanwhile, Noddy, Tessie
and Mr Plod had prepared a lovely birthday
picnic and were waiting for Whiz to come by.

"Surprise!" they shouted out as he passed.

"Happy birthday, Whiz," laughed Noddy.

"Cock-a-doodle-do!"

crowed Whiz.

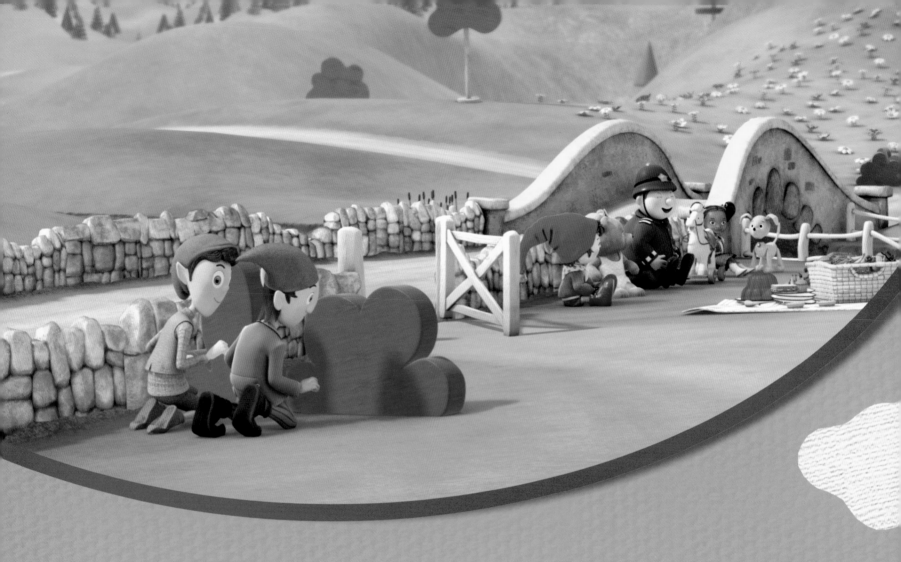

The goblins were watching from behind a bush.

"He did it!"

chuckled Sly. "That will spoil their fun!"

But to Sly's dismay,
Noddy and the others just laughed
and joined in with the crowing!

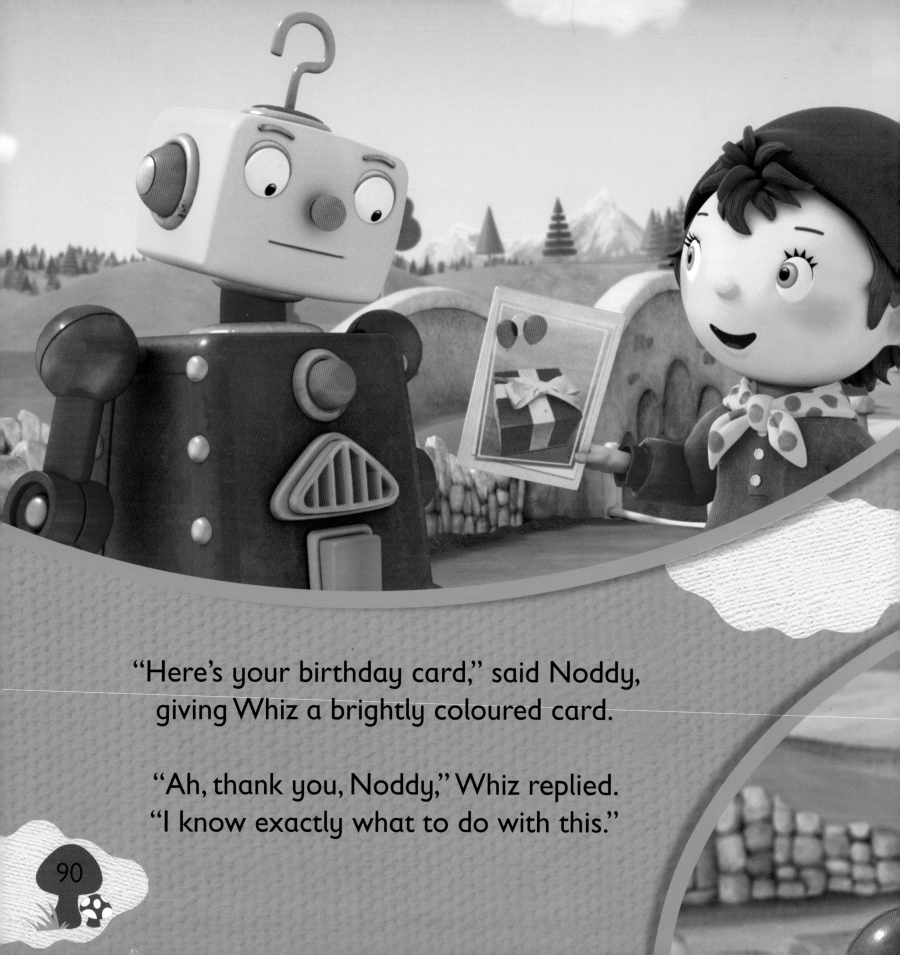

"Here's your birthday card," said Noddy,
giving Whiz a brightly coloured card.

"Ah, thank you, Noddy," Whiz replied.
"I know exactly what to do with this."

To Noddy's surprise,
Whiz took a great big bite out of it!

"Ta-da!"

Whiz cried, holding the card up in the air.

"A butterfly!" Noddy gasped, looking at the
shape Whiz had bitten. "That's lovely."

The goblins couldn't understand
what was happening.

"Something's wrong, Sly," said Gobbo.
"Every time you try to spoil the fun,
you just make it more fun!"

"Here's your present," said Noddy,
handing Whiz a pretty box.

"What am I supposed to do with my
present?" wondered Whiz.
"Ah yes, I remember!" he said,
throwing the gift into the stream!

"Ha-ha-ha!"

laughed Sly, running over to look at the present.
"I told you I'd spoil their fun!"

"Sorry Sly, you haven't ruined anything," said Noddy,
"because Whiz's birthday present is…

94